The Wizard of OZ™

The Wizard of OZ™

A novelization by M.J. Carr
Adapted from Director Victor Fleming's movie
The Wizard of Oz™

SCHOLASTIC INC.
New York Toronto London Auckland Sydney

ISBN 0-590-46993-2

12 11 10 9 8 7 6 5 4 3 2   3 4 5 6 7 8/9

Printed in the U.S.A.   40

First Scholastic printing, March 1993

The Wizard of OZ™

THE WIZARD OF OZ

adapted by M. J. Carr

1

Dorothy Gale lived in Kansas. She lived on the prairie, where the land was a dull, parched brown. It stretched flat and endless as far as the eye could see. The sky above was a cold, steel gray.

Of course, Kansas wasn't really as colorless as all that. But that's how it sometimes seemed to Dorothy. Dorothy was twelve and lived on a farm. She lived with her Aunt Em, her Uncle Henry, and her little dog Toto.

One afternoon, Dorothy hurried home from school. Toto scampered along the dusty, dirt road beside her. Dorothy was panting and out of breath. She looked back, as if she were afraid somebody might be following them.

"She isn't coming yet, Toto!" she said.

Dorothy knelt down and ran her hands through Toto's fur.

"Did she hurt you?" she asked. Despite what had happened, Toto seemed to be okay. "Come on," Dorothy said. "We'll go tell Uncle Henry and Auntie Em!"

When Dorothy reached the Gale farm, she pushed open the old wooden gate and raced toward the house. Aunt Em and Uncle Henry were outside, huddled over an old incubator.

Aunt Em was busy lifting chicks out of the incubator. She was setting them to nestle under hens set in crates nearby.

"Sixty-seven," she was counting. "Sixty-eight."

"Aunt Em!" cried Dorothy, "Aunt Em! Just listen to what Miss Gulch did to Toto!"

"Dorothy, please!" Aunt Em cut her off. "We're trying to count. This old incubator's gone bad and we're likely to lose a lot of our chicks."

"Miss Gulch hit Toto!" Dorothy persisted. "Right over the back with a rake! Just because he gets in her garden and chases her nasty old cat!"

"Don't bother us now, honey," her aunt said. She lifted out another chick.

"But Toto doesn't go in her garden every

day," Dorothy hurried on. "Just once or twice a week. And now she says she's going to get the sheriff!"

"Dorothy!" Aunt Em was exasperated. "We're busy!"

Dorothy could tell it was no use trying to talk to Aunt Em.

"Oh, all right," she said. She headed out to the barnyard. Maybe the farmhands would help her with her problem.

Zeke, Hunk, and Hickory were tinkering with the wagon.

"Zeke," Dorothy started right in, "what am I going to do about Miss Gulch? Just because Toto chases her old cat. . . ."

But Zeke didn't have time to listen to Dorothy, either. "I got them hogs to get in, honey," he said, hurrying off.

Hickory ran off after him. It seemed that no one had time for Dorothy.

Dorothy looked at Hunk. Hunk put down his hammer. "Lookit, Dorothy," he said. "You ain't using your head about Miss Gulch. Think you didn't have any brains at all!"

"I have so got brains!" Dorothy said hotly.

"Well, why don't you use them?" asked Hunk. "When you come home, don't go by Miss Gulch's place. Then Toto won't get in her garden, and you won't get in no trouble, see?"

"You just won't listen, that's all," Dorothy said. She went to the pig sty to find Zeke.

At the pig sty, Zeke was pouring slops into a trough. Dorothy climbed up on the fence that bordered the sty, and balanced on the rail.

"Listen, kid," Zeke advised Dorothy. "Are you going to let that old Gulch heifer try and buffalo ya? Have a little courage. The next time she squawks, walk right up to her and spit in her eye. That's what I'd do."

Dorothy lifted her foot. She lost her balance on the narrow fence. She tottered backwards and landed in the pigpen. Zeke leaped over the fence and pulled Dorothy out.

"Are you all right?" he asked.

"Yes, I'm all right," said Dorothy, though she was a little shaken. She looked at Zeke. His face was pale. He had to sit down. He mopped his forehead with his handkerchief.

"Why, Zeke," Dorothy laughed. "You're just as scared as I am!"

Just then Aunt Em bustled up to the pig sty.

"What's all this jabber-wrapping?" she said.

4

"There's work to be done!" Aunt Em handed out cruller doughnuts to the hungry farm-hands. "Can't work on an empty stomach," she said.

The farmhands grabbed up the fresh, warm crullers and ate them hungrily.

"And it's no place for Dorothy around a pig sty!" Aunt Em said.

That was that.

2

A unt Em started back toward the farmhouse.
Dorothy grabbed a cruller off her aunt's plate
and trailed after her.

"Aunt Em," she said. "Really. You know what
Miss Gulch said she was going to do to Toto? She
said she was going to. . . ."

"Dorothy, dear," said Aunt Em. That day, she
had neither the time nor the patience. "Stop imag-
ining things. Now, you just help us out today and
find yourself a place where you won't get into any
trouble."

Aunt Em strode back into the kitchen. Dorothy
stared miserably after her.

A place where there wasn't any trouble . . .
Dorothy wished she knew of such a place. It
wouldn't be a bit like Kansas, Dorothy thought.
It would have to be someplace far away. Some-

6

place far from the dry lands and dusty skies. Someplace over the rainbow . . .

While Dorothy was wishing that she could find this place where there wasn't any trouble, trouble was actually pedaling her way. Miss Gulch was on her bicycle, heading toward the Gale farm. Her lips were pinched. Her eyes were as steely as the sun-parched sky. She hopped off her bicycle at the gate of the farm. Uncle Henry was there, painting the fence.

"Mr. Gale," she started in, without even saying hello. "I want to see you and your wife right away about Dorothy."

"Dorothy?" Uncle Henry said. "What has Dorothy done?"

"What's she done?" Miss Gulch said indignantly. "I'm all but lame from the bite on my leg!"

"You mean she bit ya?" asked Uncle Henry, pretending not to understand.

"No!" cried Miss Gulch. "Her dog!"

"Oh," Uncle Henry said. "She bit her dog, eh?"

"No!" Miss Gulch exclaimed.

Uncle Henry set down his paintbrush and ushered Miss Gulch into the farmhouse. Aunt Em joined them in the parlor. Dorothy came in, too. She carried Toto in her arms.

"That dog is a menace to the community," said

7

Miss Gulch. "I'm taking him to the sheriff and make sure he's destroyed."

"Destroyed!" cried Dorothy. "Oh you can't! You mustn't! Auntie Em! Uncle Henry! You won't let her, will you?"

Uncle Henry fidgeted. He looked at Aunt Em. He knew that Miss Gulch meant what she said.

"If you don't hand over that dog," Miss Gulch continued, "I'll bring a damage suit that'll take your whole farm! There's a law protectin' folks against dogs that bite!"

Aunt Em tried to think of how she might calm Miss Gulch. "How would it be if Dorothy keeps him tied up?" she suggested.

"That's for the sheriff to decide," Miss Gulch sniffed. She unfolded a piece of paper. "Here's the order for me to take him. I know you don't want to go against the law."

Miss Gulch opened the lid of the basket she had brought. She pulled at Toto, trying to take him out of Dorothy's arms.

"No!" Dorothy cried. "You wicked old witch! I won't let you take him!"

But Miss Gulch got hold of Toto. There was nothing Uncle Henry or Aunt Em could do to stop her. Miss Gulch put Toto in the basket and strapped the basket to the back of her bicycle.

Dorothy ran crying to her room. Miss Gulch rode off on the bumpy road. She was smiling a smug, mean smile. She had gotten exactly what she'd come for.

As Miss Gulch pedaled down the road, she stared straight ahead of her. She didn't realize what was happening behind. Toto was pushing at the lid of the basket, trying to get free. He pushed and clawed and bit at the lid. Finally, he pushed it open and escaped.

Back in her room, Dorothy cried into the sleeve of her blue gingham dress. Suddenly, Toto leapt through her open window and into her arms.

"Toto!" cried Dorothy. "You came back!"

Dorothy hugged Toto. She realized they didn't have much time.

"They'll be coming back for you in a minute," she said. "We've got to get away!"

Dorothy packed her small suitcase and slung her traveling basket over her arm. She climbed out the window. Toto jumped out, too. The two of them slipped through the gate to the farm. They stole down the dusty road. They didn't know where they were going, or what they would find.

3

Dorothy and Toto had not been traveling long when they came upon a brightly painted carnival wagon. On the side was painted a sign. It said:

PROFESSOR MARVEL
ACCLAIMED BY THE CROWNED HEADS
OF EUROPE
LET HIM READ YOUR
PAST, PRESENT, AND FUTURE
IN HIS CRYSTAL

A man stepped out of the wagon. He was dressed in a fancy vest and a coat with a tail. It was Professor Marvel.

"Well, well," he said when he saw Dorothy and Toto and the suitcase Dorothy carried. "Houseguests, eh? And who might you be?"

Dorothy started to answer, but Professor Marvel cut her off.

"No! Don't tell me!" he said. He put his hand to his forehead as if he were trying to read Dorothy's mind. "Let's see," he said. "You're . . . traveling in disguise. No, that's not right. You're . . . going on a visit. No, no. You're . . . *running away*!"

"How did you guess?" said Dorothy. She set down her suitcase, amazed.

"Professor Marvel never guesses," he said. "He knows. Now, why are you running away?"

Dorothy started to answer, but Professor Marvel cut her off again.

"Don't tell me," he said. "They don't understand you at home. They don't appreciate you. You want to see other lands."

Dorothy stared wide-eyed at the professor. He seemed to know everything about her.

"Why, it's just like you could read what was inside of me!" she said.

"Come inside," said the Professor. "We'll consult my crystal ball."

Dorothy followed Professor Marvel into the wagon. Inside, the wagon was cluttered with trinkets, like a fortune teller's booth. Professor Marvel lit two large candles, one on either side of his crystal. He set a turban on his head. He looked into his crystal ball.

"My child," he said, "you'd better close your eyes for a moment."

Dorothy shut her eyes to concentrate. As soon as her eyes were closed, Professor Marvel reached into her basket and rummaged around. He pulled out a photograph. It was a photograph of Dorothy and Aunt Em. They were standing at the gate to the farm. When he had taken a good, long look at it, he hid the photo under the table.

"Now you can open your eyes," he said.

Professor Marvel stared into his crystal ball. Dorothy looked, too. She couldn't see a thing.

"What's this I see?" said Professor Marvel. "A house with a picket fence. And a barn with a weather vane . . ." He was describing exactly what he had seen in the photo.

"That's our farm!" cried Dorothy excitedly.

"Yes, and there's a woman," said Professor Marvel, still describing the photograph. "She's wearing a polka-dot dress. Her face is careworn. . . ."

"That's Aunt Em!" shouted Dorothy. "What's she doing?"

"Why, she's crying," said Professor Marvel.

Now he was making up his own story. "Someone has hurt her. Someone has just about broken her heart."

"Me?" Dorothy whispered. She started to feel badly that she'd decided to run away from home.

"It's someone she loves very much," said Professor Marvel.

"What's she doing now?" Dorothy asked.

"Why, what's this?" said Professor Marvel, drawing closer to the crystal. He sounded alarmed. "She's putting her hand on her heart. She's dropping down on the bed!"

"Oh no!" cried Dorothy.

Professor Marvel looked up. He shrugged. "That's all," he said. "The crystal's gone dark."

Dorothy jumped up from her chair. "You don't suppose she could really be sick, do you? I've got to get home right away! Come on, Toto!" She picked up her basket. She started down the steps of the wagon. "Good-bye, Professor Marvel!" she called back. "And thanks a lot!"

Professor Marvel watched Dorothy run down the road. The sky was darkening. The wind was gusting and kicking up leaves.

"Poor little kid," he said, shaking his head. "I hope she gets home all right. There's a storm blowing up. A whopper."

13

Professor Marvel took cover in his wagon. He knew how quickly storms could brew up in Kansas. Kansas was tornado country. Tornados had tall funnels of wind that whipped across the land. They were so powerful, they could pick up a house right off the ground.

That sort of storm promised nothing but trouble.

4

As Dorothy ran down the road, the sky grew as dark as night. The winds whipped and howled. There was indeed a tornado coming.

Back at the farmhouse, the farmhands were trying to corral the animals in the barnyard. The horses were skittish and scared. The chickens scrambled through the dust that had been kicked up by the wind. Zeke looked up at the sky.

"It's a twister!" he said. "It's a twister!"

Aunt Em was looking for Dorothy. She couldn't find her in the house. She couldn't find her in the barnyard.

"Dorothy!" Aunt Em cried frantically. "Dorothy!"

But Dorothy was still on the road, struggling against the wind, trying to get home.

Uncle Henry pulled open the door to the storm cellar.

"Come on!" he cried. "Everybody in the storm cellar!"

"I can't find Dorothy!" cried Aunt Em. "She's somewhere out in the storm! Dorothy!" she cried into the winds. "Dorothy!"

Uncle Henry looked out past the farmyard. Dorothy was nowhere in sight. He saw the tornado, though. It was only a few fields away, drawing nearer. Uncle Henry knew that if they didn't get in the cellar now, they might all be killed.

"We can't look for her now!" he said. "Come on! Get in the cellar! Hurry!"

Uncle Henry hustled Aunt Em into the safety of the cellar. Zeke and Hunk followed. They pulled the heavy cellar door shut behind them.

Just then, Dorothy and Toto reached the front gate. Dorothy headed into the winds and pushed toward the house. There was no one inside! She raced for the storm cellar. The door was shut! She tugged and tugged, but she couldn't get it open!

"Auntie Em!" she called. "Uncle Henry!"

The sound of the winds drowned out Dorothy's cries.

Dorothy and Toto ran back to the house and took shelter in her bedroom. Just then, the tornado hit the house. It blew Dorothy's bedroom window right out of its frame. The window knocked Dorothy on the head. She fell backwards onto her bed. The window knocked Dorothy unconscious.

The powerful force of the tornado lifted up the house and carried it into the sky. Dorothy opened her eyes, dazed. She sat up on the bed and looked out the window. Was she dreaming? Cows were flying by! So was a woman in a rocking chair! And two men in a rowboat!

"We must be up inside the cyclone!" Dorothy cried to Toto. Toto was hiding under the bed.

Just then Miss Gulch pedaled by on her bicycle. Dorothy blinked. Before her very eyes, Miss Gulch changed into a Witch! A dark Witch's cape billowed out behind her. On her head was a tall, pointed Witch's hat. She was no longer riding a bicycle, but a broom! The Wicked Witch threw back her head and cackled wildly.

Before Dorothy could blink again, the house was tossed wildly about by the wind. The house fell from the tornado. Dorothy grabbed onto Toto. The house was falling! It hurtled through the sky and crashed down on the land below. Bang!

"Oh!" said Dorothy.

Suddenly, all was silent.

Dorothy hugged Toto to her. She picked up her basket and tiptoed to the door. She opened the door a crack, then wider. The land outside the door was brilliant with color. Bright, tall flowers seeded the landscape. Green hills rolled under a teal-blue sky. Dorothy had never seen anyplace so colorful.

"Toto," said Dorothy. "I have a feeling we're not in Kansas anymore."

Behind Dorothy was a sound like a titter. Some little heads poked up above the bushes. The heads disappeared when Dorothy turned around.

"We must be over the rainbow!" said Dorothy as she looked all around her. It was just what she had wished for.

Dorothy ventured out of the house and down a gleaming, tile walk. Suddenly, a large, pink bubble appeared in the sky. It looked like a glistening soap bubble, though it was much larger. The bubble bounced down on the ground before Dorothy and dissolved. Inside was a woman. The woman was wearing a beautiful dress like a ball gown. Its sleeves were puffed like fairy wings. Its skirt was studded with stars. In her hand, the woman held a glittering magic wand.

"Now I *know* we're not in Kansas," exclaimed Dorothy.

5

The beautiful woman stepped toward Dorothy. "Are you a good Witch or a bad Witch?" she asked.

Dorothy didn't think the woman was talking to her. She looked around. There was no one else in sight.

"Who, me?" stammered Dorothy. "Why, I'm not a Witch at all. I'm Dorothy Gale from Kansas."

"Oh," said the woman. She pointed to Toto. "Well, is that the Witch?"

"Toto's my dog!" cried Dorothy.

"Well," said the woman. Her voice was high and musical, like bells. "I'm a little muddled. The Munchkins called me because a new Witch has just dropped a house on the Wicked Witch of the East. There's the house," she said, pointing to Dorothy's house. "And here *you* are. And that's all that's left of the Wicked Witch of the East."

Dorothy looked to where the woman was pointing. A pair of feet stuck out from underneath the house. On the feet were a pair of ruby slippers.

"And so," said the woman, "what the Munchkins want to know is, are you a good Witch or a bad Witch?"

"I'm not a Witch at all," Dorothy protested. "Witches are old and ugly!"

Again, a tiny tinkling of laughter sounded behind the bushes.

"What was that?" asked Dorothy.

"The Munchkins," said the woman, smiling. "They're laughing because *I* am a Witch. I'm Glinda, the Witch of the North."

Dorothy curtsied politely. "I beg your pardon," she apologized. "I've never heard of a beautiful Witch."

"Only bad Witches are ugly," explained Glinda. "The Munchkins are happy because you have freed them from the Wicked Witch of the East."

"What are the Munchkins?" asked Dorothy.

"The Munchkins are the little people who live in this land," said Glinda. "It's Munchkinland. And you are their national heroine, my dear."

Glinda gestured toward the bushes. "It's all

right," she called. "You may all come out and thank her!"

One by one, the Munchkins stepped out from their hiding places. They were tiny little people. One handed Dorothy a bouquet.

"You killed the Witch and we thank you," he said.

Then the mayor stepped forth. "I welcome you to Munchkinland," he said, extending his hand.

Dorothy could not believe her ears. Her house had landed on the Wicked Witch of the East! And now the Witch was dead! The Munchkins began to sing and dance with joy.

"The Wicked Witch is dead!" they cried.

As everyone was celebrating, an explosion parted the crowd. A red puff of smoke cleared from the explosion. In the midst of the smoke was an evil-looking Witch. She was staring angrily at the feet of the dead Witch. The Munchkins gasped and scattered to their hiding places.

"I thought you said the Witch was dead!" Dorothy said to Glinda. Dorothy's voice shook from fear.

"That was her sister, the Wicked Witch of the East," explained Glinda. "This is the Wicked Witch of the West. She's much worse than the other one."

"Who killed my sister?" cackled the Witch. "Who killed the Witch of the East?" The Witch pointed her long, bony finger at Dorothy. "Was it you?"

"No!" stammered Dorothy. "It was an accident! I didn't mean to kill anybody!"

"Well, my little pretty," the Witch threatened. "I can cause accidents, too!"

"Aren't you forgetting the ruby slippers?" Glinda asked her.

"The slippers!" said the Witch. "Yes! The slippers!"

The Witch reached for the ruby slippers on her sister's feet. As she did, the slippers vanished.

Glinda smiled. She pointed her wand at Dorothy's feet. The ruby slippers were on Dorothy now!

"Give me back my slippers!" demanded the Witch.

"Keep tight inside them," Glinda whispered to Dorothy. "Their magic must be powerful, or she wouldn't want them so badly."

Glinda turned to the Witch. "You have no power here," she said. "Begone before someone drops a house on you, too."

The Wicked Witch cowered at the thought. "Very well," she agreed. "But as for you," she threatened Dorothy. "I'll get you, my pretty, and your little dog, too!"

The Witch laughed an evil laugh. She twirled around. And with that, as quickly as she had arrived, she vanished in another burst of smoke and flame.

6

When the Wicked Witch was gone, Glinda called again to the Munchkins.

"It's all right," she said. "She's gone."

Glinda turned to Dorothy.

"I'm afraid you've made quite an enemy of the Wicked Witch of the West," she said. "The sooner you get out of Oz altogether, the safer you'll sleep, my dear."

"I'd give anything to get out of Oz altogether!" exclaimed Dorothy. "But which is the way back to Kansas? I can't go back the way I came."

"That's true," Glinda admitted. "The only person who might know would be the great and wonderful Wizard of Oz himself."

"Is he good or is he wicked?" asked Dorothy.

"Oh, very good," said Glinda. "But very mysterious. He lives in the Emerald City, and that's a long journey from here. Did you bring your broomstick with you?"

"No, I'm afraid I didn't," said Dorothy.

"Well, then," said Glinda, "you'll have to walk. And remember, never let those ruby slippers off your feet for a moment, or you will be at the mercy of the Wicked Witch of the West."

"But how do I start for Emerald City?" asked Dorothy.

Glinda pointed her wand to a yellow road that started at Dorothy's feet. "Follow the Yellow Brick Road," she said.

Before Dorothy could ask any more questions, Glinda's bubble reappeared. Glinda stepped in. The bubble rose into the sky and floated away.

"My!" gasped Dorothy. "People come and go so quickly here!"

Dorothy stepped onto the Yellow Brick Road. The Munchkins crowded around her.

"Follow the Yellow Brick Road!" they chanted.

Dorothy started skipping down the road. Toto bounded along beside her. The Munchkins cheered and waved good-bye.

Before long, the Yellow Brick Road branched off into another. The new road was yellow, too. Dorothy stopped at the crossroads.

"Now which way shall we go?" she wondered.

"Pardon me," said a voice. "That way is a very nice way."

Dorothy whirled around. "Who said that?" she demanded.

Behind her was a Scarecrow hanging from a pole. His face looked a little like Hunk's, from the farm. Toto barked at the Scarecrow.

"Don't be silly, Toto," said Dorothy. "Scarecrows don't talk."

The Scarecrow pointed to one road, then the other. "Of course, some people do go both ways," he said.

"Why, you did say something, didn't you?" Dorothy exclaimed.

The Scarecrow shook his head no. Then he nodded his head yes.

"Can't you make up your mind?" asked Dorothy.

"That's the trouble," said the Scarecrow. "I haven't got a brain. Only straw."

The Scarecrow pulled some straw out of his head to show Dorothy.

"It's very tedious being stuck up here all day long with a pole up your back," he said, sighing.

Dorothy reached up and tried to help the Scarecrow off his pole. He seemed to be stuck.

"If you'll just bend the nail down in the back . . . ," suggested the Scarecrow.

Dorothy bent the nail. The Scarecrow slipped off the pole and landed on the ground. Straw fell out of his jacket. The Scarecrow stuffed the straw good-naturedly back in and stood up. His legs were wobbly. He stumbled forward and took a tumble over the fence.

"Oh!" said Dorothy.

The Scarecrow sat up, grinning. "Did I scare you?" he asked hopefully.

"Of course not," said Dorothy. "I just thought you hurt yourself."

The Scarecrow's face fell. "I can't even scare a crow," he said. "I'm a failure because I haven't got a brain."

"What would you do with a brain if you had one?" asked Dorothy.

"Do?" cried the Scarecrow. "Why, I'd think of all kinds of new things! I'd think things all day long!"

"Maybe the Wizard of Oz could help you," Dorothy suggested. "I'm going to the Emerald City so the Wizard can help me get back to Kansas."

"Maybe the Wizard could give me some brains," said the Scarecrow. "Won't you take me with you?"

27

"Why, of course I will," said Dorothy.

Dorothy linked her arm in his. She and Toto and their new, straw friend set off down the Yellow Brick Road. They were going to see the Wizard. Surely, the great and powerful Wizard of Oz could help them get the things they wanted.

7

When they had been traveling a while, Dorothy began to feel hungry. Alongside the road was a grove of apple trees. Dorothy didn't know that the Witch was hiding behind a tree, watching her. She reached up into a tree to pick an apple. Much to her surprise, the tree grabbed the apple back.

"What do you think you're doing?" demanded the tree. Then it slapped her hand. "How would you like to have someone pick something off of you?"

"Oh dear," said Dorothy. This was not the sort of tree she was used to at all. "I keep forgetting I'm not in Kansas."

"I'll show you how to get apples," the Scarecrow said, running up to help her.

The Scarecrow waggled his fingers in his ears

to taunt the tree. The tree pelted him with apples. Dorothy and the Scarecrow scrambled to gather up all the apples scuttering over the ground.

As Dorothy stooped to pick up one of the apples, she noticed a foot. She looked up. The foot belonged to a Tin Man who was holding up an ax. His face looked a bit like Hickory's, from the farm. Dorothy rapped on the man's chest.

"Why, it's a man!" she said. "A man made out of tin!"

The man tried to say something. His voice was creaky and rusty.

"Oil can!" he creaked. "Oil can!"

Dorothy looked around. On the ground, not far from the man, was an oil can.

"Where do you want to be oiled first?" Dorothy asked.

"My mouth," creaked the man.

The Scarecrow picked up the can and oiled the Tin Man's mouth.

"My goodness!" said the Tin Man, flexing his jaw. "I can talk again! Oil my elbows!"

Dorothy and the Scarecrow set about oiling the Tin Man's elbows. They oiled his other joints.

"How did you ever get like this?" Dorothy asked him.

"Well," explained the Tin Man, "about a year

ago, I was chopping that tree. Suddenly it began to rain. Right in the middle of a chop, I rusted solid. I've been that way ever since."

"Well, you're perfect now," Dorothy said, to reassure him.

"Perfect?" cried the Tin Man. "Bang on my chest if you think I'm perfect. Go ahead, bang on it!"

Dorothy rapped on his chest. The rap made a hollow, echoing sound.

"It's empty," said the Tin Man miserably. "The tinsmith forgot to give me a heart."

"No heart?" said Dorothy.

"All hollow," said the Tin Man. "More than anything, I wish I had a heart. If I had a heart, I could love, like people do."

Dorothy whispered something to the Scarecrow. The Scarecrow whispered back. They had an idea.

"We were just wondering," said Dorothy. "Why don't you come with us to the Emerald City to ask the Wizard of Oz for a heart?"

"What if the Wizard wouldn't give me one when we got there?" asked the Tin Man.

"Oh, but he will!" cried Dorothy. "He must! We've come such a long way already!"

Dorothy was interrupted by a wicked peal of

nasty, cackling laughter. She looked up. On the roof of the Tin Man's cottage stood the Wicked Witch! She had them cornered now!

"You call that a long way?" sneered the Witch. "Why, you've just begun!" She looked at the Scarecrow and the Tin Man. "Helping the little lady along, are you, my fine gentlemen? Well, stay away from her!" she snapped.

The Wicked Witch waved her hand and conjured up a blazing ball of fire. She threw it at the Scarecrow.

"Want to play ball?" she laughed.

The Scarecrow leaped out of the way of the fireball. It was sparking near his straw.

"Look out!" he cried. "Fire! I'm burning!"

The Tin Man ran up and swatted at the fire with his tin hat to smother it. On the roof, the Witch cackled wildly. Then she vanished in a puff of red smoke. She'd done enough damage for the day.

"I'm not afraid of her," said the Scarecrow, getting up and dusting himself off.

"I'll see that you get to the Wizard, Dorothy," agreed the Tin Man.

"Oh," said Dorothy. "You're the best friends anybody ever had. It's funny, but I feel as if I've known you all the time."

The Scarecrow offered his arm to Dorothy.

"To Oz!" he said.

"To Oz!" echoed the Tin Man.

Dorothy and the Scarecrow and the Tin Man set off once again down the Yellow Brick Road. Toto scampered happily beside them.

8

Dorothy and her friends traveled farther down the Yellow Brick Road. Around them, the woods grew thick and dark.

"Oh," said Dorothy. "I don't like this forest! It's dark and creepy! Do you suppose we'll meet any wild animals?"

"We might," said the Tin Man.

"Animals that eat straw?" asked the Scarecrow, alarmed.

"Some," nodded the Tin Man. "But mostly lions and tigers and bears."

"Lions and tigers and bears!" cried Dorothy. "Oh my!"

The three friends peered out into the darkness. They didn't know what was lurking there. Suddenly, they heard a roar. It was a lion's roar!

"Oh!" cried Dorothy.

From behind the brush, a lion leaped out at Dorothy and her friends. He gave a ferocious roar. He stood up on his hind paws and started boxing.

"Put 'em up, put 'em up!" he challenged the Scarecrow and the Tin Man. "I'll fight ya both together. I'll fight ya with one hand tied behind my back. I'll fight ya with my eyes closed."

"Here, here," said the Tin Man. "Go away and let us alone!"

"Scared, huh?" said the Lion. He punched at the Tin Man. "Get up and fight, ya shiverin' junk-yard," he said. "Put ya hands up, ya lopsided bag of hay!" he taunted the Scarecrow.

Toto scampered forward, barking and nipping at the Lion's heels.

"I'll get you, peewee!" roared the Lion.

Dorothy jumped forward and grabbed up Toto. She slapped the Lion on the nose.

"Shame on you!" she cried.

The Lion started crying.

"What did ya do that for?" he whimpered. "I didn't bite him!"

"No, but you tried to," lectured Dorothy. "It's bad enough picking on a straw man, but when you go around picking on poor little dogs . . ."

The Lion sniffed up his tears. "Well, you didn't have to go and hit me, did ya? Is my nose bleedin'?"

"My goodness, what a fuss you're making!" said Dorothy. "Why, you're nothing but a big coward!"

"You're right," snivelled the Lion. "I am a coward. I haven't any courage at all. I even scare myself."

"Oh," said the Scarecrow. He felt sorry for the Lion. "That's too bad." He turned to Dorothy. "Don't you think the Wizard could help him, too?"

Dorothy studied the Cowardly Lion. "I don't see why not," she said. "Why don't you come along with us? We're on our way to see the Wizard now. To give the Tin Man a heart. And the Scarecrow a brain. I'm sure he could give you some courage."

The Lion wiped his paw across his nose.

"Gee, that's awfully nice of ya," he said. "My life has been simply unbearable. Look at the circles under my eyes. I haven't slept in weeks."

"Oh, well it's all right now," Dorothy comforted him. "The Wizard'll fix everything."

Dorothy linked her arm in the Lion's.

"Come on!" she said.

The Scarecrow and the Tin Man linked up as well. Now there were four friends traveling together down the Yellow Brick Road, four friends trying to get to the Emerald City.

Dorothy and her new friends were excited. They knew they must be close to the Emerald

City now. They didn't know that the Wicked Witch was watching them, still. She was in the tower of her dark castle, looking into her crystal ball. Beside her sat Nikko, one of her Winged Monkeys.

"Aha!" said the Wicked Witch as she watched the friends skipping down the road. "So you won't take my warning, eh? All the worse for you, then. I'll take care of you now instead of later!"

The Witch mixed a beaker of poison. She was going to try to prevent Dorothy and her friends from getting to the Wizard.

"Hah!" she laughed. "When I gain those ruby slippers, my power will be the greatest in Oz!"

The Witch held the beaker of poison close to the crystal ball.

"And now my beauties," she cackled. "Something with poison in it. Poison that's attractive to the eye, soothing to the smell."

In the crystal ball appeared a field of poppies. They were bright red. Their poison looked pretty.

"Poppies will put them to sleep," said the Witch. She ran her fingers menacingly over the crystal ball. "Sleep," she cooed. "Sleep. Now they'll sleep. . . ."

9

Dorothy and her friends were indeed close to the Emerald City. As they marched down the road, they could see it in the distance. Its spires were green and glistening, as beautiful as they'd imagined.

"There's Emerald City!" cried Dorothy. "We're almost there at last!"

"Let's hurry!" said the Scarecrow.

"Let's run!" agreed Dorothy.

Between the friends and the Emerald City stood a field. It was a field of poppies, the one that the Witch had poisoned with her potion. To get to the Emerald City, the friends had to cross the field.

"Come on!" shouted the Scarecrow as he bounded through the poppies.

"Hurry!" shouted the Tin Man.

Everyone was running. Dorothy and Toto lagged behind. Dorothy stopped and put her hand to her forehead. The poison of the poppies was making her drowsy.

"What's happening?" she said. "I can't run anymore. I'm so sleepy."

"Here," said the Scarecrow. "Give us your hands and we'll pull you along."

But Dorothy couldn't go any farther.

"I have to rest," she said. She looked around for her dog. "Toto," she said. "Where's Toto?"

Toto was at her feet, sound asleep amidst the poppies. Dorothy sank down beside him. Her eyelids were heavy. She fell fast asleep as well.

"You can't rest now!" exclaimed the Scarecrow. "We're almost there!"

Beside him, the Lion was yawning.

"Come to think of it," the Lion said drowsily, "forty winks wouldn't be bad."

The Scarecrow and the Tin Man grabbed the Lion up by the arms to keep him alert and awake.

"We ought to try and carry Dorothy," said the Tin Man.

They let go of the Lion. The Lion fell flat on his back. He had fallen fast asleep, too!

"This is terrible!" said the Scarecrow.

The Scarecrow and the Tin Man tried to lift up Dorothy. She wouldn't budge. Suddenly, the Scarecrow realized what was happening.

"This is a spell!" he said.

"It's the Wicked Witch!" cried the Tin Man. "What will we do?"

He looked around frantically for help.

"Help!" shouted the Tin Man. "Help!"

"It's no use screaming at a time like this," said the Scarecrow. "Nobody will hear you." Nonetheless, he started screaming, too. He didn't know what else to do. "Help!" he shouted even more loudly. "Help!"

Though no one was in the poppy field, someone did hear them. It was Glinda, the Good Witch of the North. She knew how to help Dorothy and her friends. She knew how to undo the Witch's spell.

Glinda waved her wand. Suddenly, the sky above the poppy field was full of snowflakes. They fell softly on the poppies. They fell on Dorothy and Toto and the Lion, sleeping in the field. The Scarecrow looked up at the sky in wonder.

"It's snowing!" he said. "Maybe that'll help!"

Dorothy stirred among the poppies. She opened her eyes. The cold, wet snow was counteracting the drug of the poppies! The Lion woke up and sat bolt upright. He looked at the snow all around him.

"Unusual weather we're having, ain't we?" he said.

Dorothy stood up and blinked the sleep from her eyes. She looked at the Tin Man.

"Look!" she said. "He's rusted!"

The snow had indeed rusted the Tin Man.

"Give me the oil can! Quick!"

As Dorothy was oiling the Tin Man's joints, the Wicked Witch looked back into her crystal ball. She saw the snow falling. She saw Dorothy, Toto, and the Lion wide awake once again.

"Curse it!" she cried furiously. "Somebody always helps that girl!"

The Witch summoned Nikko.

"Shoes or no shoes," she said, "I'm still great enough to conquer her! And woe to those who try to stop me!"

In the field, Dorothy and her friends once again linked arms. They tramped through the snow-covered field to get back on the Yellow Brick Road.

"Come on!" said Dorothy. "Let's get out of here! Emerald City is closer and prettier than ever!"

Back in the Witch's tower, the Wicked Witch had grabbed up her broomstick.

"Ha!" she laughed.

She jumped on her broomstick and flew out the window.

"To the Emerald City!" she cackled. "As fast as lightning!"

10

Dorothy and her friends skipped up to the gate of the Emerald City. The gate was closed. Dorothy rang the bell. A man peered out from a little, round window high atop the door.

"Who rang that bell?" he demanded.

"We did!" all four friends said together.

"State your business," said the doorman.

"We want to see the Wizard!" chorused the friends.

"The Wizard!" scoffed the doorman. He'd never heard such nonsense. "Nobody can see the Great Oz! Nobody's ever seen the Great Oz! Even I've never seen him!"

"Please, sir," pleaded Dorothy. "I've *got* to see the Wizard. The Good Witch of the North sent me."

"Prove it," barked the doorman.

"She's wearing the ruby slippers she gave her," said the Scarecrow.

The doorman looked down. There were the ruby slippers, right on Dorothy's feet.

"So she is," said the doorman. "Why didn't you say that in the first place? That's a horse of a different color!"

The doorman opened the gate.

"Come in," he invited them.

Inside the gate was a glittering, glistening city. As Dorothy and her friends entered, a horse-drawn carriage pulled up beside them.

"Take you anywhere in the city," offered the cabby.

"Would you take us to see the Wizard?" asked Dorothy.

"The Wizard!" The cabby laughed. "First I'll take you to a little place where you can tidy up a bit."

Dorothy and her friends hopped into the carriage. As they did, the horse in front turned a rich shade of purple.

"What kind of horse is that?" Dorothy gasped. "I've never seen a horse like that before!"

"No," said the cabby. "And never will again, I fancy. There's only one of him and he's it. He's the Horse of a Different Color you've heard tell about."

Dorothy watched the horse, amazed. As she watched, the horse turned red, then yellow. The Emerald City was proving to be quite magical a place indeed.

The cabby drove Dorothy and her friends to a shop. The sign over the door read, *Wash & Brush Up Company*. Inside, the Scarecrow was attended by a group of men. They took out his old straw and stuffed his suit of clothing full with fresh, new straw.

The Tin Man got a polishing. His old tin body was brushed and shined. The Lion got his nails filed. Dorothy got her hair curled. The Wash & Brush Up Company got everyone looking fresh and clean. Now the four friends were ready to see the Wizard.

As Dorothy and her friends stepped out of the shop and onto the city square, a loud noise startled them. They looked up into the sky. The people of Oz crowded around, looking, too. In the sky, the Witch was flying overhead on her broomstick.

"It's the Witch!" cried Dorothy. "She's followed us here!"

Behind the Witch's broomstick was a trail of

smoke. The smoke was spelling something out.

"Surrender Dorothy," read the Lion.

"Dorothy?" said the people of Oz. "Who's Dorothy!"

Dorothy bit her lip. The Witch meant her!

"The Wizard will explain it," said a woman.

"To the Wizard!" said a man.

The people of Oz ran off to find the Wizard. They wanted him to explain.

"Whatever shall we do?" said Dorothy.

"We'd better hurry if we're going to see the Wizard!" said the Scarecrow.

Dorothy and her friends ran off, following the crowd. This was not going to be quite the introduction they'd hoped for.

11

By the time Dorothy and her friends got to the gates of the Wizard's palace, the people of Oz were crowded there. They were shouting and clamoring to see the Wizard. In front of the gates was a guard.

"Here! Here!" cried the guard. "Everything is all right. The Great and Powerful Oz has got matters well in hand. There's nothing to worry about. You can all go home."

Dorothy and her friends pushed their way through the crowd.

"If you please, sir," Dorothy spoke up, "we want to see the Wizard right away. All four of us."

The guard shook his head. "Orders are: Nobody can see the Great Oz. Not nobody, not nohow!"

"But she's Dorothy," said the Scarecrow.

"Dorothy?" The guard recognized the name. That was the name the Wicked Witch had written in the sky. "The Witch's Dorothy?" he said. "That makes a difference. Wait here. I'll announce you at once!"

The guard marched inside the gate of the palace. Dorothy and her friends could scarcely believe their luck.

"Did you hear that?" said the Scarecrow. "He'll announce us at once!"

Soon they would all see the Wizard. Soon they would get the things they had come for.

"I've as good as got my brain!" said the Scarecrow.

"I can fairly hear my heart beating!" said the Tin Man.

"I'll be home in time for supper!" said Dorothy.

The Lion puffed up his chest. "In another hour, I'll be King of the Forest!" he boasted. "Long live the King!"

Dorothy and the Scarecrow and the Tin Man bowed to the Lion, as if he were already King. The Lion strutted back and forth proudly. Soon, if the Wizard was able to help him, he'd be brave. And courageous. He wouldn't be afraid of anything.

"Not nobody, not nohow!" he said. "I'd show everyone who was King of the Forest!"

Just then, the guard came back out of the palace.

"The Wizard says go away!" he said abruptly. With that, the guard strode back into the palace and slammed the door shut behind him.

"Go away?" chorused the four friends. They stared at the door that had slammed in their faces.

"Oh," Dorothy moaned.

"Looks like we came a long way for nothing," said the Scarecrow.

Dorothy sank down on the steps of the palace. "And I was so happy," she said miserably. "I thought I was on my way home."

Dorothy felt worse than she had ever felt. She started to cry. Her friends gathered around to comfort her. The Scarecrow pulled a handkerchief from Dorothy's basket and handed it to her. Dorothy sniffed and snivelled.

"Don't cry, Dorothy," said the Tin Man. "We're going to get you to the Wizard."

"We certainly are," the Scarecrow assured her.

Dorothy could hardly speak through her tears. "Auntie Em was so good to me," she said, weeping. "And I never appreciated it. Running away and hurting her feelings. . . . Professor Marvel said she was sick. She may be dying! And it's all my fault!"

Dorothy didn't know it, but the guard was watching her through a window in the door. When he saw Dorothy crying, he started to cry, too. He started sobbing as hard as Dorothy.

"Oh, please don't cry anymore," he said, wiping away his tears. "I'll get you in to see the Wizard somehow! Come on! I had an Aunt Em myself once."

The guard flung open the doors to the palace. The four friends piled in. In front of them was a long hallway. It had a high, arched ceiling. Dorothy and her friends did not see a person, nor did they hear a sound. The four of them crept cautiously down the hallway, not knowing what they would find at the other end.

12

Halfway down the hallway, the Lion stopped short.

"Wait a minute, fellas!" he said. "I was just thinkin'. I really don't want to see the Wizard this much. I better wait for you outside."

He turned on his heel to go, but his friends grabbed hold of him.

"What's the matter?" asked the Scarecrow.

"Oh, he's just ascared again," said the Tin Man.

The Lion started crying. He clutched his tail for comfort. Dorothy tried to reassure her friend.

"Don't you know the Wizard's going to give you some courage?" she said.

"I'd be too scared to ask him for it," bawled the Lion.

"Well, then we'll ask him for you," offered Dorothy.

"I'd sooner wait outside," said the Lion. His friends grabbed him, so he wouldn't try to escape again. With the Lion's paws firmly in their hands, they continued down the hall.

At the end of the hall were two tall doors.

"Come forward!" boomed a voice.

The Lion covered his eyes with his paws.

"Tell me when it's over," he said, shaking.

The four friends entered the Wizard's chamber. At one end was a huge throne. Pots of fire sparked and flamed at either end. No person sat on the throne. Instead, a large, vaporous head seemed to float above it in the air.

"Look at that!" cried the Lion. "I want to go home!"

"I am Oz, the Great and Powerful," announced the head. "Who are you?"

None of the four could say a word. They huddled together, quaking in fear.

"Who are you?" Oz demanded again, this time louder.

Dorothy's friends pushed her forward as spokesperson.

"If you please," started Dorothy. Her legs were shaking. Her voice was quavering. "I am Dorothy, the Small and Meek. We've come to ask you. . . ."

"SILENCE!" boomed Oz. Flames sparked up from the pots of fire. Smoke billowed. "The Great and Powerful Oz knows why you have come! Step forward, Tin Man!"

The Tin Man froze in place. Dorothy shoved him forward.

"You dare to ask me for a heart!" accused Oz. "You clinking, clanking, clattering collection of caliginous junk!"

"Yes, sir," said the Tin Man, backing away.

"And you, Scarecrow," continued Oz, "have the effrontery to ask for a brain? You billowing bale of bovine fodder!"

"Yes, Your Honor. I mean, Your Wizardry," said the Scarecrow, trembling.

"And you, Lion!" said Oz. He seemed to be waiting for some sort of answer. "Well?"

The Lion tried to speak, but fear once again stopped him. He fainted in front of the throne.

Dorothy rushed up to help her friend. She was furious at the Wizard.

"You ought to be ashamed of yourself!" she scolded. "Frightening him like that, when he came to you for help!"

"Silence, whippersnapper!" commanded Oz. "The beneficent Oz has every intention of granting your requests!"

"What?" asked Dorothy. It seemed to her quite the opposite.

"But first," said Oz, "you must prove yourselves worthy by performing a very small task."

The four friends leaned forward hopefully. Maybe they still had a chance.

"Bring me the broomstick of the Witch of the West," commanded Oz.

"B-b-b-but," stuttered the Tin Man, "if we do that, we'd have to kill her to get it!"

"Bring me the broomstick!" Oz commanded. "And I'll grant your requests. Now go!"

"But what if she kills us first?" asked the Lion.

"I said GO!" boomed Oz.

Oz's voice echoed off the walls of the hall and reverberated through the room. The Lion was terrified. He turned tail and ran out of the room.

"Aaaaahhh!" he wailed.

The Wizard had said "Go," and go he did. He dove straight through the window with a crash.

13

To get to the castle of the Witch of the West, Dorothy and her friends had to pass through a dark and eerie woods.

HAUNTED FOREST, said a sign. *WITCH'S CASTLE 1 MILE. I'D TURN BACK IF I WERE YOU!*

The Lion read the sign. The woods around him were scary and creepy. He'd be only too happy to turn back. . . .

Two owls blinked down at the friends from one tree. Two crows stared down from another. Their eyes glowed like fire in the dark.

"I believe there're spooks around here," said the Scarecrow.

"Spooks!" scoffed the Tin Man. "That's ridiculous!"

"Don't you believe in spooks?" asked the Lion.

"No!" said the Tin Man.

Just then, something lifted the Tin Man up off the ground, though there didn't seem to be anyone or anything anywhere near. Whatever it was dropped him back down on the path. Crash!

"Tin Man!" cried Dorothy.

"Are you all right?" cried the Scarecrow.

The Lion clutched onto his tail, more afraid than ever.

"I do believe in spooks," he chanted superstitiously. "I do. I do."

It was, however, not a spook that had lifted up the Tin Man. It was the Witch. She was watching the four friends through her crystal ball. She was cackling loudly.

"You'll believe in more than spooks before I've finished with you!" she squawked.

The Witch went to her window. Nikko was poised at the ledge. Around him were many more Winged Monkeys. They were the Witch's army.

"Take your army to the Haunted Forest," the Witch commanded Nikko, "and bring me that girl and her dog. Do what you like with the others, but I want her alive and unharmed! Take care of those ruby slippers," she added. "I want those most of all!"

The Winged Monkeys thronged to the window, excited and chattering.

"Fly!" the Witch commanded. "Fly!"

Suddenly the sky swarmed with flying monkeys. Their wings flapped loudly as they made their way toward the Haunted Forest. When they saw Dorothy and her friends, they swooped as one, down from the sky. Dorothy and her friends looked up at the monkeys in terror.

"Help!" shrieked Dorothy. "Help!"

Two monkeys dove at Dorothy and chased after her. More monkeys jumped on the Scarecrow, pulling out his straw. Monkeys seemed to be everywhere, vicious and attacking. The monkeys who chased Dorothy grabbed her by the arms and flew her up into the sky, back toward the Witch's castle.

"Toto!" Dorothy screamed. "Toto!"

The little dog looked up at Dorothy, as she kicked and screamed, skimming the tops of the trees. Toto barked furiously. One of the monkeys grabbed him up and tucked him under his arm. He flew off after Dorothy.

The monkeys' job was finished. The rest of the army took off toward the castle, leaving the Scarecrow, the Tin Man, and the Lion helpless on the ground.

"Help!" the Scarecrow shouted.

The Tin Man ran over to his friend. The Scarecrow was flat on his back. His straw had been scattered every which way.

"They tore off my legs," said the Scarecrow. "And threw them over there. Then they took my chest out and threw it over there."

"They sure knocked the stuffin' out of ya, didn't they?" said the Lion.

"Don't just stand there talking!" cried the Scarecrow. "Put me back together!" His friends ran to gather up straw. "We've got to go find Dorothy!" commanded the Scarecrow.

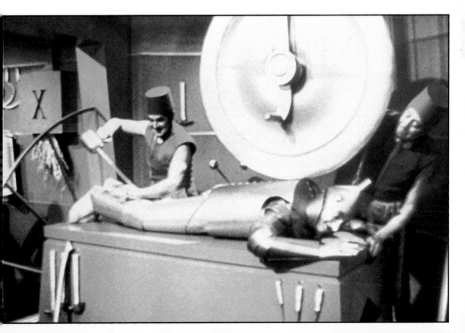

14

High atop a mountainous rock sat the Witch's castle. The Witch was in her tower. She clutched Toto on her lap.

"What a nice little dog," she sneered.

The Witch dropped Toto into a basket and closed the lid. She handed the basket to Nikko. Then she turned to Dorothy.

"And you, my dear," she said. "It's so kind of you to visit me in my loneliness."

"What are you going to do with my dog?" Dorothy cried anxiously. "Give him back to me!"

"Certainly," said the Witch. "When you give *me* those slippers."

"But the Good Witch of the North told me not to!" said Dorothy.

"Very well," said the Witch. She smiled an evil

smile. She tossed a look to Nikko. "Throw that basket in the river and drown him!" she ordered.

"No!" cried Dorothy desperately. "No! Here! You can have your old slippers!"

The Witch leered at the slippers. She knelt down to tear them off Dorothy's feet. As she touched the slippers, though, they sparked and flashed. Pain shot through the Witch's hands.

"Ooooh!" she shrieked.

"I'm sorry. I didn't do it," said Dorothy. "Can I still have my dog?"

"No!" shouted the Witch. "Fool that I am! I should have remembered! Those slippers will never come off as long as you're alive!"

The Witch squinted, scrutinizing Dorothy.

"But that's not what's worrying me," she said. "It's how to do it. These things must be done delicately, or you hurt the spell."

Across the room, Toto pushed his way out of the basket. He scrambled across the floor and out the door.

"Catch him, you fool!" the Witch shouted at Nikko.

Nikko took off after Toto, but Toto was quick and agile. He streaked down the steps of the tower. When he got to the entrance of the castle, the drawbridge was just starting to rise. Toto raced to the edge of the drawbridge. He jumped off the bridge and over the moat, landing safely on the opposite shore.

Nikko had summoned the guards of the Witch's castle, guards called Winkies. The Winkies ran down the drawbridge, chasing after Toto. They carried long spears and hurled them at Toto on the ground below. Dorothy watched the chase from the window high up in the Witch's tower.

"Run, Toto!" she urged. "Run!"

Toto dodged the Winkies' spears and scrambled for cover behind the rocks of the mountain.

"He got away!" cried Dorothy, relieved.

The Witch whirled around to Dorothy.

"Which is more than you will!" she threatened. "Drat you and your dog! You've been more trouble to me than you're worth. But it'll soon be over now!"

The Witch grabbed up a tall hourglass. She turned it over and set it down on the table.

"You see that?" she said, as the sand in the hourglass began sifting to the bottom. "That's how much longer you've got to be alive. And it isn't long, my pretty, it isn't long! I can't wait forever to get those shoes!"

With that, the Witch stormed out of the room and locked the door behind her.

Dorothy didn't know what to do. She sank down next to the crystal ball.

"I'm frightened," she whimpered. "I'm frightened, Aunt Em."

Just then, a picture appeared in the crystal ball. It was Dorothy's Aunt Em! She was looking all around, looking for Dorothy.

"Dorothy!" she was calling. "Dorothy, where are you? We're trying to find you. Where are you?"

Dorothy called out to the image of her aunt.

"I'm here in Oz," she cried. "I'm locked up in the Witch's castle. I'm trying to get home to you, Aunt Em!"

But Aunt Em didn't seem to see Dorothy, or even to hear her. The image of her worried face faded from the crystal ball.

"Oh Auntie Em!" Dorothy cried. "I'm frightened! Come back!"

As she was crying, another image appeared in the crystal ball. It was the face of the Witch. Dorothy shrunk from the crystal in horror.

"Auntie Em! Auntie Em!" the Witch cried,

mimicking Dorothy. "I'll give you Auntie Em, my pretty!" she cackled.

The Witch threw back her head and laughed a terrifying laugh. On the table beside Dorothy, sand streamed through the hourglass.

Time was running out.

15

As the sand ran through the hourglass, Toto scrambled down the rocks of the mountain. He headed back toward the forest. In a clearing were the Tin Man and the Lion. They were stuffing straw back into the Scarecrow, who still lay on the ground.

"Look!" said the Tin Man. "There's Toto! Where'd he come from?"

"Don't you see?" said the Scarecrow. "He's come to take us to Dorothy!"

The Scarecrow scrambled to his feet. "Come on, fellas!" he cried.

Toto barked excitedly and led them to the trail. The Scarecrow, the Tin Man, and the Lion followed as the little dog clambered up the steep, rocky mountain. The Tin Man lost his footing. He grabbed onto the Lion's tail.

"I hope my strength holds out," the Lion said.

"I hope your *tail* holds out," answered the Tin Man.

At the top of the peak was a turreted castle. It stood dark and menacing against the sky.

"What's that?" asked the Lion.

"That's the castle of the Wicked Witch!" said the Scarecrow. "Dorothy's in that awful place!"

"I hate to think of her in there," said the Tin Man. "We've got to get her out!"

The three friends eyed the castle from the safety of the rocks nearby. As they did, the Winkie Guards marched into view. They were dressed in long, heavy coats and tall helmets. In their hands they held sharp spears. It looked as if it would be impossible for the friends to get past the guards and into the castle.

"I've got a plan how to get in there," said the Scarecrow.

"Fine," jeered the Lion. "He's got a plan."

"And you're going to lead us," the Scarecrow informed him.

"Me?" said the Lion. The Lion gulped.

But before the Scarecrow could explain his plan, the three friends were ambushed by three Winkie Guards. The Guards had seen the intruders and had snuck up behind them. They pounced on the friends and wrestled them down behind the rocks.

A terrible scuffle ensued. It looked as if the friends were doomed. When the scuffle quieted, three Winkie helmets poked up above the rocks. Had the friends lost the fight?

No! The helmets now belonged to the Scarecrow, the Tin Man, and the Lion. They had felled the Winkies and taken their clothes. Now they had a perfect disguise in which to enter the castle of the Witch!

"Come on," said the Scarecrow. "I've got another idea."

They climbed down the rocks that ringed the castle. Toto ran at their heels. The rest of the Winkie Guards were falling into formation, marching back over the drawbridge and into the castle. The three friends fell in line behind them and marched right in. When they were safe inside the castle, they ducked behind a wall. The Winkie Guards marched off.

"Where do we go now?" asked the Tin Man.

Toto bounded up the steps. He turned and barked at the friends.

"There!" cried the Scarecrow. Toto was trying to lead them to Dorothy!

The three friends scrambled up the steps that led to the Witch's tower.

At the top of the steps was a door. It led to the Witch's tower room. The door was locked. Toto scratched and barked.

"Dorothy!" cried the Scarecrow. "Are you in there?"

Inside the room, Dorothy ran to the door.

"Yes, it's me!" she cried. "She's locked me in!"

"We gotta get her out!" cried the Lion. "Open the door!"

They unbuckled their heavy Winkie coats and threw off their helmets.

On the table, inside the room, the sand in the hourglass was running low.

"Hurry!" cried Dorothy. "Please hurry! The hourglass is almost empty!"

The Tin Man raised his ax and aimed it at the wood of the door.

"Stand back!" he ordered.

The Tin Man began chopping. He chopped with every bit of strength he had.

16

As the last grains of sand slipped through the hourglass, the Tin Man broke through the door. Dorothy flew into the arms of her friends. She grabbed Toto and hugged him.

"Oh, Toto," she cried. "I knew you'd come!"

"Hurry!" cried the Scarecrow. "We've got no time to lose!"

The four friends raced back down the long staircase that led to the entrance of the castle. The entrance doors were open. They were in luck!

But as the friends ran up to the doors, the doors slammed in their face. A wild peal of laughter echoed through the hall. It was the Witch. She was standing at the top of the stairway, watching them. She was sure she'd trapped them now.

"Going so soon?" she said. "I wouldn't hear of

it. Why, my little party's just beginning!"

The Witch held up the empty hourglass. Their time was clearly up.

As the Witch laughed her mad laugh, a large battalion of Winkies raced into the hall. Their spears were raised. They surrounded the four friends and closed in on them, step by step.

"Don't hurt them right away," coached the Witch. "We'll let them *think* about it first."

The Winkies closed in. The Scarecrow thought hard. Above the Winkies was a chandelier. It was held up by a rope that was fastened to the wall. If only he could think of a way to cut it loose . . .

In a flash, the Scarecrow grabbed the Tin Man's arm. The Tin Man's ax sliced through the rope. The chandelier crashed from the ceiling and fell on the Winkies. In the confusion, the four friends broke through the line of guards.

"Seize them, you fools! Stop them!" cried the Witch.

The Winkies chased after Dorothy and her friends. The friends ran up the stairs.

"There they go!" shouted the Witch. "Now we've got them. Hurry! Hurry!"

When the four reached the top of the tower,

they came to a narrow parapet that led to a second tower.

"This way! Come on!" cried the Scarecrow.

But as they reached the second tower, they were cut off by the Witch. The friends turned to run back the way they'd come. But, from that direction, Winkies were running toward them. Enemies were coming from every direction! The friends were truly trapped.

"Well," laughed the Witch. "Ring-around-the-rosy! Pocket full of spears! Thought you'd be pretty foxy, didn't you? Well, the last to go will see the first three go before her."

Dorothy trembled. The Witch was talking about her.

"And her mangy little dog, too!" cackled the Witch.

The dark room was lit by torches that lined the walls. As the friends watched, the Witch lifted her broomstick and touched it to the flame. The broomstick started blazing. She poked it menacingly at the Scarecrow.

"No!" cried the Scarecrow.

The Scarecrow jumped to escape the fire, but it was too late. The Witch touched the broomstick to his straw. The Scarecrow's arm was flaming!

"Help!" he cried. "I'm burning!"

Dorothy looked around frantically. Beside her was a bucket of water. Dorothy grabbed up the bucket and tossed the water on the flames.

"Don't touch that water!" shrieked the Witch.

The water doused the fire. It also hit the Witch, splashing her full in the face. As it did, the Witch began shrinking.

"You cursed brat!" she cried. "Look what you've done! I'm melting! Melting!"

As the four friends looked on, the Witch shriveled before their very eyes. She melted down to nothing. In a few short moments, all that was left of the Witch was her black Witch's cloak and pointed cap.

"She's dead," one of the Winkies murmured. "You killed her."

Dorothy was afraid that the Winkies would attack her to take revenge.

"I didn't mean to kill her," she protested.

Instead of attacking Dorothy, though, the Winkies dropped to their knees.

"Hail to Dorothy!" they cried. "The Wicked Witch is dead!"

Once again, Dorothy was a heroine.

"The broom," Dorothy asked. "May we have it?"

The leader of the Winkies handed Dorothy the broom.

"Here. Take it with you," he said.

"Oh, thank you!" cried Dorothy. "Now we can go back to the Wizard! Now we can tell him the Wicked Witch is dead!"

17

When Dorothy and her friends arrived back in Oz, they were ushered into the Wizard's throne room. The vapory head of Oz hovered over the throne, just as it had when they'd been there before.

"Can I believe my eyes?" Oz boomed. He sounded angry. "Why have you come back?"

Dorothy stepped forward. She laid the broomstick at the foot of the throne.

"Please, sir," she said. "We've done what you told us. We've brought you the broomstick of the Wicked Witch of the West. We melted her."

"Oh, you liquidated her, eh?" chuckled Oz. "Very resourceful."

"Yes, sir," said Dorothy. "So we'd like you to keep your promise to us."

"Not so fast!" shouted Oz. "I'll have to give the

matter a little thought. Go away and come back tomorrow!"

"Tomorrow?" cried Dorothy. "I want to go home *now*!"

As the head of Oz boomed back at them, Toto ran to a curtain hanging in a corner of the room. Two feet poked out from under the curtain. Toto grabbed the curtain in his mouth and tried to tug it back.

"Come back tomorrow!" the head of Oz was shouting.

"If you were really great and powerful," Dorothy talked back, "you'd keep your promises."

Just then, Toto succeeded in pulling back the curtain. Behind the curtain was a small booth. In the booth was a man. He was pulling levers and talking into a microphone. He was the one making the head of Oz talk! Oz was not a real Wizard at all!

The man tugged the curtain out of Toto's mouth and closed it back around himself.

"Pay no attention to that man behind the curtain," he said into the microphone. The words looked as if they were coming from the vapory head over the throne. "The Great Oz has spoken!"

Dorothy walked up to the curtain and yanked it back. The man behind the curtain was slight and ordinary looking. He looked a bit like Professor Marvel from Kansas.

"Who are you?" Dorothy asked.

The man puffed up his chest and spoke into the microphone. "I am the Great and Powerful Wizard of Oz," he said.

"You are?" said Dorothy. "I don't believe you."

"I'm afraid it's true," the Wizard said, humbly now. "There's no other Wizard except me."

"You humbug!" cried the Scarecrow.

"That's exactly what I am," the man admitted.

"Well what about the heart that you promised the Tin Man?" asked the Scarecrow. "And the courage that you promised Cowardly Lion?"

"And the Scarecrow's brain!" cried the Tin Man.

The Wizard sighed. "Anyone can have a brain," he said. "That's a very mediocre commodity. Back where I come from, we have seats of great learning. Universities, we call them. Men go there to become great thinkers. When they come out, they think great thoughts. With no more brains than you have," he told the Scarecrow.

"But they have one thing you haven't got," he went on. "A diploma!"

With that, the Wizard reached into a little black bag he had in his booth. He pulled out a diploma and handed it to the Scarecrow.

75

"You are now a Doctor of Thinkology," he said.

The Scarecrow put his finger to his head and rattled off a complicated mathematical formula.

"Oh joy!" cried the Scarecrow. "I've got a brain!"

Next, the Wizard moved on to the Lion.

"As for you, my fine friend," he said, "you're under the unfortunate delusion that because you run from danger, you have no courage. You're confusing courage with wisdom. Back where I come from, we have men who are called heroes. They have no more courage than you have. But they have one thing that you haven't got. A medal!"

The Wizard reached into his black bag once again. He pulled out a medal and pinned it to the Lion's chest.

"You are now a member of the Legion of Courage," he announced.

The Lion dug his toe sheepishly into the ground.

"Shucks, folks," he said. "I'm speechless."

Now it was the Tin Man's turn.

"As for you, my galvanized friend," said the Wizard. "You want a heart. You don't know how lucky you are not to have one. Hearts will never be practical until they can be made unbreakable."

"I still want one," said the Tin Man.

"Back where I come from," said the Wizard, "there are men who do nothing all day but good deeds. Their hearts are no bigger than yours. But they have one thing you haven't got. A testimonial."

From the black bag, the Wizard pulled a heart-shaped watch and chain.

"I present you with a small token of our affection and esteem," he said, handing the watch to the Tin Man. "And remember. A heart is not judged by how much you love, but by how much you are loved by others."

"It ticks! It ticks!" cried the Tin Man.

Dorothy looked at the presents the Wizard had bestowed on her friends.

"They're all wonderful," she said.

"Hey!" cried the Scarecrow. "What about Dorothy?"

"Yeah!" said the Lion. "Dorothy next!"

Dorothy peered down into the Wizard's bag. She didn't believe the Wizard could help her.

"I don't think there's anything in that black bag for me," she said sadly.

18

The Wizard looked at Dorothy.

"You force me into a cataclysmic decision," he said. "The only way to get Dorothy back to Kansas is for me to take her there myself."

"Oh, will you?" exclaimed Dorothy. "Could you?"

"Child," said the Wizard. "I'm an old Kansas man myself. I worked as a premier balloonist with the Miracle Wonderland Carnival Company. Until one day, when an unfortunate phenomenon occurred. The balloon drifted away and failed to return to the fair."

"Weren't you frightened?" asked Dorothy.

"Petrified!" admitted the Wizard. "Then suddenly, the wind changed and the balloon floated down into the heart of this noble city. I was instantly acclaimed Oz, the first Wizard deluxe! Times being what they were, I accepted the job. But I kept my balloon," he said. "And in that balloon, Dorothy, you and I will return to Kansas."

* * *

The Wizard led the four friends into the center of Emerald City Square. In the center of the square was a platform. On the platform was the Wizard's balloon. Dorothy gathered Toto into her arms and stepped into the basket of the balloon with the Wizard. Her friends held down the ropes that tethered the balloon to the ground.

All the people of Oz gathered around to cheer. They wanted to bid good-bye to their great and powerful wizard.

"My friends," announced the Wizard. "I am about to depart. Until I return, the Scarecrow, by virtue of his highly superior brains, shall rule in my stead. He will be assisted by the Tin Man, by virture of his magnificent heart. And the Lion, by virtue of his courage. Obey them as you would me."

Dorothy hugged Toto. She was almost home now. But before the balloon could take off, Toto spotted a cat in the crowd. Toto growled and pricked up his ears. He wriggled free from Dorothy's arms and jumped out of the basket.

"Toto!" cried Dorothy. "Come back!"

Dorothy scrambled out of the basket and chased after her dog.

"Don't go without me," she shouted back to the Wizard. "I'll be right with you!"

When the Scarecrow and the Lion saw Toto escaping in the crowd, they dropped the ropes to the balloon to try to help catch him. The balloon started to rise. The Tin Man clutched onto the last rope, but he couldn't hold the balloon down by himself.

"Help me!" cried the Tin Man. "The balloon's going up!"

The balloon jolted upward. The Wizard lurched. He grabbed onto the rim of the basket.

"This is highly irregular," he said. "Absolutely unprecedented. Ruined my exit."

The balloon started rising. It rose higher and higher. Dorothy stood on the ground, staring helplessly up at the balloon.

"Come back!" she shouted. "Come back! Don't go without me!"

"I can't come back!" the Wizard called back. "I don't know how it works!"

As the balloon trailed off in the sky, the Wizard waved good-bye to the people of Oz. Dorothy's eyes welled with tears.

"Now I'll never get home!" she cried.

It seemed to Dorothy that she'd now have to stay in Oz forever.

19

Dorothy's friends were upset to see her so sad. They gathered around to comfort her.

"Stay with us, Dorothy," said the Lion. "We all love ya. We don't want you to go."

"Oh," Dorothy said sadly. "That's very kind of you, but this could never be like Kansas. Auntie Em must have stopped wondering what happened to me by now."

She buried her head against the Scarecrow's shoulder.

"Oh, Scarecrow, what am I going to do?" she wailed.

Just then, a beautiful pink bubble floated above Emerald City Square.

"Look!" said the Scarecrow. "Here's someone who can help you!"

The bubble floated over the heads of the crowd. The crowd stepped back to make room for it.

When the bubble drifted down, Glinda stepped out. She waved her magic wand. The Good Witch of the North had returned to help Dorothy.

Dorothy curtsied before the beautiful Witch.

"Will you help me?" she asked.

Glinda smiled at her little Kansas friend.

"You don't need to be helped any longer," she said sweetly. "You've always had the power to go back to Kansas."

"I have?" asked Dorothy.

"Then why didn't you tell her before?" asked the Scarecrow.

"Because she wouldn't have believed me," said Glinda. "She had to learn it for herself."

"What have you learned?" the Scarecrow asked Dorothy.

Dorothy thought a moment.

"Well," she said. "I think that if I ever go looking for my heart's desire again, I won't look any farther than my own backyard. Because if it isn't there, I never really lost it to begin with."

"Is that right?" Dorothy asked Glinda.

"That's all it is," Glinda answered.

"But that's so easy," said the Scarecrow. "I should have thought of it *for* you!"

"And I should have felt it in my heart," said the Tin Man.

"No," explained Glinda. "She had to find it for herself."

Glinda waved her wand down at the ruby slippers which still held tight to Dorothy's feet.

"And now those magic slippers will take you home in two seconds," she said.

"Toto, too?" Dorothy asked.

"Toto, too," said Glinda, smiling.

"Now?" asked Dorothy. At the very thought, her heart flooded with joy.

"Whenever you wish," answered Glinda.

Dorothy wanted to get home as soon as she could. But that meant she would have to leave her friends. She turned to bid them good-bye.

"It's going to be so hard to say good-bye," she said. "I love you all."

The Tin Man was crying. Dorothy wiped away his tears.

"Don't cry," she said. "You'll rust dreadfully."

"Now I know I've got a heart," said the Tin Man. "Because it's breaking."

Dorothy rose up on her toes to kiss the Lion.

"Good-bye, Lion," she said. "I know it isn't right, but I'm going to miss the way you used to holler for help before you found your courage."

The Lion snivelled up his tears.

"I never would have found it if it hadn't been for you," he told her.

Finally, Dorothy turned to her first friend. She threw her arms around the Scarecrow and hugged him tightly.

"I think I'll miss you most of all," she whispered in his ear.

"Are you ready now?" asked Glinda.

"Yes," said Dorothy. She had said her good-byes.

Dorothy took Toto in her arms. She waved his little paw.

"Say good-bye, Toto," she said. She took a breath. "I'm ready," she said.

"Then close your eyes," Glinda instructed. "And tap your heels together three times . . ."

Dorothy closed her eyes. She clicked the heels of her ruby slippers.

"And think to yourself," said Glinda. " 'There's no place like home. There's no place like home.' "

Dorothy repeated the words after Glinda. "There's no place like home."

Suddenly, her head felt dizzy. It felt as if the world around her were spinning. Dorothy squeezed her eyes shut tighter and chanted the magic words.

20

When Dorothy came to, she was lying in her bed. She was in her bedroom, in Kansas. Auntie Em was leaning over the bed, pressing a cool, wet cloth to Dorothy's forehead.

"Wake up, honey," cooed Auntie Em.

Dorothy blinked at the room around her.

"There's no place like home," she continued to chant deliriously. "There's no place like home."

"Dorothy, dear," said her aunt. She peered worriedly at Dorothy. "It's Auntie Em."

Dorothy stared at her aunt, trying to focus. It was indeed Auntie Em! And Uncle Henry was there, too!

"Hello!" cried a voice. "Anybody home?"

It was Professor Marvel. He poked his head in Dorothy's window.

"I just dropped by because I heard the little girl got caught in the big storm," he said.

He spied Dorothy lying in bed.

"Well, she seems all right now," he said.

"Yeah," said Uncle Henry. "She got quite a bump on the head. We kinda thought there for a minute she was going to leave us."

"But I *did* leave you," Dorothy tried to explain. "That's just the trouble. And I tried to get back for days and days . . ."

"There, there," said Auntie Em, trying to quiet the little girl. "Lie quiet now. You just had a bad dream."

"No," Dorothy insisted.

Just then, Dorothy noticed Hunk, Hickory, and Zeke. The farmhands had been keeping watch over her, too.

"Sure," said Hunk, trying to help quiet Dorothy. "Remember me? Your old pal Hunk?"

"And me?" asked Hickory.

"You couldn't forget my face, could ya?" chimed in Zeke.

Dorothy thought back on all she had seen.

"No, it wasn't a dream," she said, trying to piece together all that had happened to her. "It was a place."

She looked at the faces of the farmhands. They looked like the faces of the friends she'd met in Oz.

"And you were there. And you. And you," she said, pointing to the farmhands.

Professor Marvel chuckled from the frame of the window. He looked so much like the Wizard. . . .

"And you were there," she insisted.

"Sure," said Hunk, trying to humor her.

Everyone laughed.

Dorothy tried to think back. She didn't know how any of this could be.

"But you couldn't have been there, could you?" she said, confused.

"Oh, we dream lots of silly things," Aunt Em said to appease her.

"No, Aunt Em," Dorothy tried to explain. "This was a real truly live place. And I remember that some of it wasn't very nice. But most of it was beautiful! Just the same," she said, "all I kept saying to everybody was, 'I want to go home.' And they sent me home!"

Dorothy looked out at her family and friends. They were staring at her blankly.

"Doesn't anyone believe me?" she asked.

"Of course we believe you, Dorothy," Uncle Henry said gently.

Toto jumped up on the bed next to Dorothy.

"Oh, but anyway, Toto, we're home!" cried Dorothy.

She gazed out at all the warm, friendly faces that surrounded her.

"And this is my room," she said, trying to orient herself. "And you're all here. And I'm not going to leave here ever, ever again! Because I love you all!"

Dorothy was once again safe in the farmhouse in Kansas. She grabbed Toto to her and hugged him tightly.

"Oh, Auntie Em," she cried fervently. "There's no place like home!"